Well Deserved

Miko Christiaansen

Well Deserved

Miko Christiaansen

ISBN: 978-1-951522-23-0

MIKO AND RAVEN: AN INTRODUCTION

by John Urbancik

I have struggled with how to approach this introduction. Because, though the subject matter of this novella is absolutely brutal, Miko Christiaansen is so much more than the trauma behind this story.

She asked me to help her see this through to the end, and I was honored. A little frightened, too, because the nature of the story is outside of my personal experience and outside of the things I generally write. Because this was never going to be my story to tell.

It was Miko's. It's the story of thousands, even millions, of other women. It had to be told. It is at times savage, always honest, and also heartbreaking.

The existence of this book tells me everything I need to know about Miko Christiaansen – not as a writer, not even as a woman, but as a human being and as a friend. She's courageous. She attacked her personal traumas in the most direct possible way. And she did so with unflinching intensity.

Granted, I already knew all this about Miko. I've seen her strength. Her compassion. I honestly don't remember the first time we met, but I distinctly remember when we truly connected, a couple of years later, sharing a moment of our individual sorrows.

In this story, she deals with some of her personal sorrows and the trauma behind them. This in no way diminishes what she's experienced, but I think it was definitely a means of exorcising the worst of it. It's a story shared by many women. It's a story not understood by enough men. It resonates on a visceral, emotional level in a disturbing yet beautiful, straightforward way.

This is a telling of Raven's story.

There are many villains in this story. Some are obvious, and you will grow to despise them for the things they do. Some go unnamed – and though not actively complicit, they also do bad things – sometimes with good intentions. As readers, we only see from Raven's perspective, so we don't know the truths of the struggles faced by other people in her life.

It's safe to say that Raven's perspective, as she tells her story, is skewed, biased by the events of her life that led her to this place, warped by the volatile emotions of a teenager – the same emotions we all, at one point, dealt with – amplified by events over which she has no control.

In that way, maybe Raven is a villain in her own story. You can decide that yourself after you're introduced to her, after you see what's done to her, after you see what she does.

Miko will handle that introduction.

My purpose is to introduce you to Miko Christiaansen: the strong and vibrant woman; the merciless, unflinching author; the thoroughly involved mother of four wonderful children; and a true, genuine friend who showed up for me in my time of need despite that, when she most needed someone, no one showed up for her. Still, she survived. She didn't just grow, she excelled. And in this book, she's sharing a story of what might have been, under other circumstances, and what never should have been at all.

–John Urbancik
March 2026

DEDICATION

To my sister Michelle; my daughters Tarynn, Serenity, and Melody; my son Corey; and my nieces Cali, Mekayla, Stephanie and Freya. I love you all so much. Everything I do, I do for the nine of you.

Also to my Grammy: everything I do in life is in hopes that you are proud of me. I miss you every day. I love you.

Well Deserved

Miko Christiaansen

PROLOGUE

Let's get one thing straight. I am not a serial killer. I'm a Goddamn vigilante. I don't have a psychosis. I don't have a need to kill *innocent* men. These bastards are far from innocent. There are no voices instructing this rage. This is all me. These sick fucks deserve everything they get and then some. And I don't do it at random. The government provides the good citizens of America with a website pointing us right to their dwellings. It's almost as if they gave me the green light to go ahead and destroy these mother fuckers.

Maybe I'm getting ahead of myself. Shall I start from the beginning? My name is Raven and I'm 17 years old. I grew up in Eureka, California with my single mother who worked way too hard and spent all of my time with my best friend. Marie and I first became best friends in Kindergarten. She was the pretty and shy girl. I was the loud and obnoxious one. We complimented each other well. Life was simple and easy for us on the playground, after school, and on weekends. Summer vacations, we played dolls and hide and seek, soccer, volleyball, even jump rope. Marie had one doll in particular she always carried around back then. I think she called it Ana. We read the same books, watched the same movies, and when we each played alone, we did so together. We listened to the same music and crushed on the same musicians.

Those first six years, it was gonna be us against the world forever. Then, about four years ago, pretty and shy Marie attempted suicide. Pills. Because she just couldn't take it anymore. Apparently, mommy dearest had a pervert for a boyfriend who liked to sneak into her room at night and do things you just do not do to prepubescent 13-year-old little girls. I made her throw up the pills. I've always known what to do. And she gave me details. Too many details.

That's gotta be the first time I felt rage. It grew hot inside me. What was I supposed to do with this? Marie cried it all out, and every tear just made me madder. So yeah, I snapped! I went into the kitchen, grabbed the sharpest butcher knife I could find, swore Marie to secrecy, and dragged her along to find him.

In the bathroom attached to the bedroom he shared with Marie's mom, we found him. She'd moved him in, and he'd wasted no time starting up with Marie. She'd been getting quieter, but I had never noticed. I thought the bruises were from us running around all over the place.

And now, he was piss ass drunk, getting urine on the toilet seat. He was scrawny, like he never really ate much. Just drink, sleep, and repeat. I didn't give him a chance to notice me, I just bashed him over the head with the hairdryer crowded onto the edge of the sink. Like all the rage I felt exploded out of me in a strength well beyond my age. I remember staring in the mirror after hitting him. I hardly recognized myself. My chest heaved. Hair disheveled, pupils dilated...I was a mess; a beautiful mess. Exhilaration running rampant in my veins, I ran out of the room to find some rope.

Marie was no help at this point. She watched, she cried, and I let her. But those tears stopped as I got to work with the rope and she just stared at him the whole time.

By the time he came to, I had him tied to the bed and facing the mirror on Marie's mother's dresser. Which was no easy feat and took a lot of effort, but lucky me, he wasn't much heavier than me to begin with...taller, yes, but scrawny. Still, I worked up sweat shoving him across the floor, and I needed Marie's help to get him on the bed. After that, I made her go. She didn't need to see what I wanted to do. She needed to be at my house, instead. I was already thinking ahead.

I had his pants down, and got to work carving into his nasty, saggy, hairy balls. I'd gagged him so my innocent 13-year-old ears didn't have to hear the vulgarity that I am almost positive he was spewing. I hadn't expected that much blood, but I kept good and clear of most of it. I made quick work of cutting his testicles from their sack. But that wasn't exactly where I wanted my fun to take place. No, the things Marie told me led to my favorite part of this endeavor. I shoved the blade up his ass. Straight in. As deep as the knife could go. I thought there'd be more resistance. I didn't think there'd be that much blood. When I twisted the knife, his garbled screams felt like music to my ears. After ripping it from his ass and spraying blood everywhere, I yanked his head back by his hair and, so he could see it in the mirror, sliced his throat, ear to ear.

An insane amount of blood got everywhere. It just poured out of him. I thought it would flow forever, and I thought he would spasm like a flea all tied down with nowhere to go, but he didn't. I was splattered in blood and even shit, but it didn't faze me. I was energized and hyper-focused, like I had just done a line of coke, I jumped away from his warm corpse. I'd just fucking killed this guy! I saved my best friend...hell, I saved the *world* from a pedophile. I was fucking badass!

I bet you're all wondering how this didn't lead back to Marie and me. Easy answer? We had a solid alibi of being in my room, at my house, the whole time, because that's where Marie took off to. Thankfully, that's the only murder Marie knows about, I never wanted her in on anything, just in case I did get caught. Still haven't been caught, though. Four years, same M.O., and those idiots have no idea that I, Raven Harold, Senior at Eureka High School, am the one slaughtering all these sick, disgusting, totally deserving pedophiles.

CHAPTER ONE

"Hey, would you turn that up?" I call out to Marie from the kitchen where I am finishing the touches on our after school coffee and blueberry muffins. My favorite song was playing on the stereo in the living room. When Slipknot's "Killpop" plays, you blare it.

The volume slowly increases. Marie isn't a big fan of my type of music these days, but being my best friend, she has to deal. When I walk back into the living room, Marie is quietly fretting over something. Her nails are freshly bitten and the crease between her eyebrows is furrowed in consternation. Her hair is mussed from running her fingers through it one too many times. She never hides her distress well.

"Okay, spill." I set down the muffins, hand over her coffee, and plop down on the couch, careful not to jostle my own aromatic goodness and drench myself in it. People claim it's alcohol abuse to spill beer or liquor. We claim it's coffee abuse to spill the heavenly brown lifesaver.

"What do you mean?" she asks, trying to adjust her posture to look as though nothing is wrong. Taking a big gulp of her coffee, she turns to look out the window, avoiding eye contact with me.

"You're biting your nails and staring off into space. We've been best friends for ten years, now tell me what's bugging you."

"Nothing. Just..." she sighs "Okay, so what would you do if I told you my mom *actually* found a good job?"

I smile. "I'd say about fucking time..."

Looking down at her hands, she quietly adds "154 miles east of here...in Shasta Lake."

"Uuuuuh...." I don't know how to respond. I don't believe it. "Yeah, no."

"Rave, it's a good job and stable." Marie rushes on before I interrupt. "We move tomorrow!"

"What?! You have *got* to be kidding me!?" I realize I'm yelling and try to calm down. "How long have you known?"

She whispers. "For about a month now."

"Why didn't you tell me sooner?"

"I didn't know how to."

We sit in silence for a while. I'm starting to get all jittery, like if I don't get up and do something I might break down. So I jump up, tell Marie some excuse about forgetting something of some sort somewhere, and I run out the door. As I'm climbing into my car a notification goes off on my phone.

New Sex Offender Listed in The Area

This is just what I need. A release. I map the address and drive there to scout the area. As I am waiting, I pull out my tablet to do some research on my new friend: 47 years old, just released from serving four years for molesting his 7-year-old stepdaughter. *Who the fuck can even find it possible to feel sexual attraction to a little girl so young?*

Besides the point. Apparently, he lives alone. Makes for easy prey.

I go for the sweet and innocent approach and knock on his door. He answers after a minute or so. "Can I help you?" He looks me up and down, in a spine numbing manner.

I force my lips to tremble, as if I'm truly upset by my situation. "My car broke down and I can't find my phone."

I recently discovered this approach. These perverts practically trip over themselves trying to let me into their home. They never see the crowbar hidden in the arm of my shirt. "Can I come in to call my dad to pick me up?"

He nods and leads the way up the hall. I never bother with small talk. I already know everything I need to know about them. I quietly lock the door behind me. He gets two, maybe three steps before I bum rush him from behind with a crowbar and smash his head. He drops pretty easily. I work quickly to tie him up and run to find a loose mirror. His house looks like any other house, a few plain pieces of furniture, cheap framed photos he bought at some discount store on the wall in the hallway. All their places steal from the same boring floor plan, as though outside their proclivities they have nothing else in their souls. The bathroom is sparse. Contains almost nothing but soap, a pair of towels, and a razor. I find the mirror hanging on the back of the door.

When he comes to, I've already got his balls sitting on the floor in front of him in a puddle of blood. He screams and struggles against the rope, but I have done this so much I'm not phased in the slightest. I brandish the knife from behind him, smile at him via the mirror and make sure he sees the blade, then shove it up his ass so hard and fast I even surprise myself.

Must be my anger at Marie leaving me.

I only twist the knife a time or two before yanking it out. I usually relish this part. Reminds me every time of my first kill. Of course, today, that just makes me angry. Marie might not remember it, but we shared that first kill.

I jump on his back and slice his throat. Blood splashes the mirror and his eyes glaze over. I give him one last smile through the mirror, drop his head, and wait for him to stop blubbering before going to the bathroom sink to rinse the knife real good with bleach.

I've gotten good at this. I hardly get any pedo blood on my hands and none on my clothes.

I leave calmly.

I find it strange how, even in the middle of the day, no one has ever seen me leaving the scene of the crime. The police are convinced they're looking for a woman in her 40s who has probably been molested or raped as a child. This isn't the first pedo *murder*. They've been all over the news for four years now. One would think they'd come up with a new profile. Lucky for me, they haven't.

The next morning, in Lit class, everything hits me. I'm just sitting there, jamming to 'Monster' by Stitched Up Heart through my earbuds and writing a poem for class, when suddenly my chest tightens up on me.

White Rose Turns Black

—Time goes by slowly
sun begins to rise
tears stain the pillow
blood stains the knife
white rose turns black
piece by piece
tear by tear
pain begins to flow away

—With the snap of a finger
you curse her
time stands still
blood will spill
with the breath of a word:
"suicide"

—Lies and heartaches
white rose turns black
newspaper headings
tears held back

—Scars on the heart
tears in the wind
words unspoken
so solid, so true
yet still so blue

White rose turns black

The seat in front of me is achingly empty. There is no Marie bouncing in her seat, turning around to read what I'm writing and tell me it's way too dark. A tear falls from my eye as I grab my phone to text her,

"I miss you, come back." As soon as I hit the send button a text comes in from her,

"Just breathe, Rave. Breathe." It's like she knows how I'm feeling at this very moment. I'm trying to breathe slowly and ignore those feelings when some random jackass sits in her seat. The odor that emanates from this insidious creep makes me tear up more than Marie's absence. The words that come out of my mouth next are not at all polite, "*Hey*, until you learn what *deodorant* is for, do *not* sit in front of me or I might have to stab you in the aorta with this pencil."

Instantly, I know I am fucked. One, that was

said way too loud, and two, Ms. Hogan is standing just two chairs back from me.

"*Miss* Harold, would you care to tell me why you think it's appropriate to threaten another student in my class?"

Oh boy. "Truth?" I ask, keeping my voice as quiet and even as I can.

"Enlighten me."

This is going to suck. I am not one for having a filter when I feel anxious. "Well, since you asked, he stinks. He stinks so bad I am tearing up. But also, he is sitting in Marie's seat. I know she's gone, but I also know that we were assigned seats in this class and his seat is four rows that way." I point to my left by the windows.

She stares at me for a moment as if I suddenly grew two heads, then she directs me to go to the hallway where we can finish this conversation.

As I'm walking out the door, I hear her directing Mr. Stank-ass to his assigned seat. I can only chuckle. But it isn't long before she's next to me attempting to explain her understanding of how I feel. "...but for the love of God, stop bullying people as a release for being upset."

By way of getting this to be a done subject I simply nod, apologize, and follow her back into class. With Mr. Stank now back where he belongs, I can go back to my quiet sulking, moody, teenage ways of feeling distraught about my best friend suddenly disappearing from my life; oh the joy.

CHAPTER TWO

To take my mind off of everything, I go for a run. Don't knock it. When you're a female teenage vigilante, stamina is highly important. Just as important as those mixed martial arts classes. Taking down pedophiles is not as easy as I may have made it seem. One time, when I was about 15, there was this one guy, fresh from jail, buff as hell, and not so easy to subdue. I *actually feared* for my life for the first time while doing what I do. He stopped my crowbar. No one ever stopped the crowbar before. Usually, metal hits head and body drops to the floor. But no, not with this guy. Metal hit shoulder instead. He turned and got a hand on it. And once he had a hand on it, there was no way I was gonna be able to get another swing at him. I didn't have the strength. I didn't have the leverage. Another half minute of that struggle, and it would've been me dropped to the floor.

Eventually, I had to stab him in the jugular with my knife. I got so much more blood on me than at any other time. It came out of his throat like a fountain. And I couldn't look away from his eyes. Those eyes condemning me as if I was the evil one here until they went glassy. And those glassy fucking eyes still stared at me!

I considered toying with him post death, but that didn't seem even close to as much fun as when they're alive and screaming. That was the one time my M.O. changed. I even thought about giving all this up. Instead, that kill made me sign up for the mixed martial arts classes. Two years of that and I no longer had to fear for my life with anybody.

Blaring Flyleaf's "I'm So Sick" in my ears from the music app on my phone, I round the corner and run straight into someone.

"Whoa!" the guy says, steadying me by grabbing on to my shoulders. Now, you gotta understand this. Murdering pedos has never stopped me from being attracted to the opposite sex. The sickos I kill don't even register as human in my eyes. But this guy, he is all man.

Gorgeous blue eyes, a dirty blonde that looks mostly brown until it hits just the right light, and then out pops those natural blonde streaks. About 5'9, maybe 5'10, muscular but not in a grotesque way. A smile that could make even the strongest woman swoon and have to change her panties. Defined simply: walking sex.

Breathless, I quickly apologize. "I am *so* sorry, I was in the zone and wasn't paying attention."

"No harm, no foul," he says with a laugh. Letting go of my shoulders, he gives me one last good look and a heart-stopping smile before continuing on his way. I don't know why, but I suddenly get this feeling that this is not the first time we have met in my lifetime and it will not be the last. Who the fuck is this guy, and why do I feel as if my life is never going to be the same?!

— — —

Later, after I am showered and climbing into bed, I get a message from Marie telling me she plans to come back this weekend for my 18th birthday. As much as I want to be hype, I can't be. What's one weekend when she is just going to leave again? She is the only person who grounds me when my crazy flag begins to fly. I need a new friend. How do I make new friends? Marie has been my best and only friend for ten years. She knows things no one will ever know. *FUCK*! Tears start to fall from my eyes and as I curl into a ball. Leaving her message on read, I fall asleep feeling completely alone for the first time in my life.

— — —

Checking the clock, I see I am definitely going to be late meeting Marie at the bus station. Why is this guy taking so long to wake up? Slapping him across the ass, I yell, "Wake the hell up, Darell! It's time to play."

The fucker has slept through all the fun stuff – strangely enough. Normally I wait for them to awaken before diving in, but I am on a time crunch dammit. Finally he starts to stir. Perfection.

Excitedly, I grab him by the back of his ponytail and leap onto his back. Yanking back his head by his hair, I blow him a kiss in the mirror and slice open his throat. The blood sprays across our reflection, giving me that familiar high I just cannot explain. As his body drops to the floor, I stand up and head to the kitchen to bleach the knife and put it back exactly where I found it in the knife block on the counter. No use carrying around a murder weapon.

The blade I carry is for emergencies.

I exit through the kitchen door to the fence in the back that will lead to my car. I make quick work of removing my hoodie and track pants as I cross the yard and hide them in the secret lock box I installed underneath the floor of the passenger seat. The odor shield should keep them well hidden while Marie is with me this weekend and should make people think I'm masking the smell of weed.

As I drive to retrieve Marie from the bus station, I think back to not long after we were cleared of having anything to do with her mother's dead boyfriend's murder. Marie was so elated. I was just plain surprised. How could they not have pinned it on me? I had been practically on the verge of admitting it to the cops there and then.

There was zero proof that I was in my room with Marie at that time. My own mother hadn't even seen me come home with Marie. Admittedly, we'd decided it would be best for Marie to sneak in through the window and then go downstairs to ask if my mom could make us some cookies while we studied. My mother didn't see me until after the murder had been timed to have happened. But since she'd seen Marie, and Marie claimed to have seen me, it was an open and shut situation.

We were presumed innocent. I don't believe I had ever seen Marie so happy as in that moment of clarification. Jay was dead and her best friend – who had done it – was not in jail. She turned up her little *girl power* music so fucking loud and danced around her room for hours. I just sat there watching, daydreaming already of how I could do it again. I had opened a Pandora's box, so to speak, and was completely unwilling to close it.

Approaching the bus station, I see Marie bouncing up and down as she waves me to the open parking space she's standing near. The thing about Marie is that her happiness is contagious. Once the drama of the dead pedo was over, she became one of the happiest girls I had ever met.

As I climb out of the car she launches herself at me, hugging me tighter than anyone would expect from such a tiny person.

"OH MY GOD! Raven! You have no idea how much I have missed you.!" She's screaming the words, and throwing them out an ungodly speed.

"Things are absolutely nutso in my new high school. I definitely think most those people are related, that's how small that town is. It is totally ridiculous." She pauses only long enough for half a breath. "But please, tell me, how are you? Are you staying out of trouble? Are you ready to celebrate your birthday? I cannot believe you are eighteen. Just a few more months and I will be too. Hey! I should come back again for my birthday or maybe you can come to me—"

I slap my hand over her mouth. "Stop. *Breathe.*" I say it on a giggle as I grab her hand and pull her along, "Let's go see where the rest of your bags are." Beaming, Marie tags along behind me.

Once in the car, Marie hits me with the third degree again, "So, Rave, what's new?"

"Not a whole lot. Met a pretty hot guy while jogging the other day. Thinking I might have to see about bumping into him again, now that I'm 18."

I feel her staring at me in utter shock but I keep my eyes on the road.

"Who is he? What does he look like? I didn't even know you could notice when a guy was hot..."

That last one stings a bit. "Gee, thanks Mar..."

We grow quiet after that. Something is different for us. It hasn't even been that long since she left, and yet things aren't as easy as they have always been. There is a sudden uneasiness I'm not used to. I don't know if it's her or me. But it can't be me. I'm not the one who left.

I try to ease the sudden tension by throwing a

question or two at her. "So did you get all settled at your new school? Make a new best friend?"

Wait. No, that won't kill any tension. What if she says yes? She stares at me as if I suddenly sprouted a second head, "Geez, Rave, possessive much? Why would you even ask that? Sometimes I feel like you are completely ridiculous and clueless." There's nothing I can say to that. She's never called me out on my shit in this way before. I'm not a big fan, to be completely honest. The distance has changed us, I can feel it. Tensions I have never before noticed between us are suddenly very obvious. So thick you could cut it with a knife.

Miko Christiaansen

Chapter Three

We go through the motions. We convince some college boys to buy us a bottle of Crown Apple. College boys are so easy to manipulate. Just suggest a little bit of something you'll never actually give them. Half of them are pedos, anyway, and I should probably just take out the lot of them.

They do have their uses, though. It's good, because it tastes like shit, burns going down, and allows me to blissfully ignore the fact that Marie isn't telling me shit about her replacement friends in the new school.

I know she's got some. She names one girl. I can't remember the name. They have a class together and she listens to one of our bands and she wears black lipstick and writes secret poems in a little black book. Marie insists the girl won't show her. I know she's lying.

I show her *White Rose Turns Black*. Of course I do. I've shown her every stupid little poem I've scribbled in the past ten years, and I don't think I was making much poetry before that.

Her eyes trace over the words. She says she loves it. But then we're looking up weird shit online to make us laugh, dancing to Disturbed and Papa Roach and Matchbox 20. All the divorced dad rock we always listened to. She doesn't bring me anything new. She doesn't say anything specific about my poem. Doesn't ask if I've made any new friends since she abandoned me.

Instead, past midnight, we're looking up dumb shit on the internet to laugh at, but it all feels forced, like we have to do this because we always have, and I'm sure she'd rather be home again with her new friends. She talks too fast, delays too long, laughs too loud.

I find myself checking for a pedo alert every few minutes. Any excuse to get some air. And there's nothing. Absolutely nothing. Kinda pisses me off, actually.

We don't fall asleep. We get so drunk we pass out. Which is good. Because neither of us is gonna wake up before noon.

The tension between us lasts the whole weekend. I can sense she's hiding something and I know she can tell I know. We aren't the same. It hasn't even been a week and already our friendship has changed for the worse. After what seems like the longest, most awkward, weekend, it's finally Sunday. I drive her back to the bus station, in silence, and we make open ended promises to keep in touch. What the fuck has happened to our easy friendship? Will we ever be the same?

I need to clear my head, so I go home and change into my running gear and hit the streets. No need to lie to myself, I am so looking for Mr. Walking Sex. I take the same path as before and I am not disappointed. Sitting on a bench not far from where I first bumped into him is the cutie himself. I come to a halt and prepare myself to talk to him. I don't mean to sound conceited, but I grew up to be pretty good looking. My teeth are straight and white, eyes blue as the sky above, wavy long raven black hair (which I'm told is why my mom named me Raven), perky little breasts, and an ass that would make a grown man cry. I'm *hot.* There is no way this guy is going to turn down my advances.

Sitting next to him on the bench, I clear my throat to grab his attention. Looking up from his book, an easy, and gorgeous, smile comes to his lips.

"Out for another run?" he asks.

The sound of his voice brushes over me like silk. *What is it about this guy?* I steady myself, so as not to show how affected I am by him.

"Yeah, well, what better way to stay in shape than a good run?"

He chuckles, which is also like silk across my skin. "You're right there. I'm Dominick..." He reaches over to shake my hand. "Or Nick, if you prefer."

I grab his hand. "I'm Raven, nice to meet you."

We sit like that for a minute, hand in hand, looking at each other. Something about this man makes me feel reckless, like I could jump his bones right here on the bench. Or fall so deeply in love, I crash and burn with no one and nothing left to pick up the shattered pieces of what remains of my demented little soul.

Nick is the first to release the hold of both hand and eyes. “Well Raven, I should probably let you get back to running.”

As he goes to stand and leave, I grab his hand again, not willing to let him go. “Wait, I don’t normally do this, but would you like to go get some lunch with me?”

I see the war of thoughts in his mind. He looks at me so intensely my heart begins to speed up. *Please say yes, please say yes.*

“Sure, why not?” He uses my hand on his to pull me to my feet. The action surprises me and I slam up against him.

He holds me there for only a moment, my hands on his chest, lips inches from lips. Eyes staring into eyes. I don’t believe I have ever been this turned on before. Releasing his hold on me, he steps back and ushers me to lead the way. I feel his eyes on my ass as I walk towards the restaurants on Main Street. If nothing else, this could be the start of an amazing fuck.

I’m not an eighteen-year-old virgin. I lost my v-card a couple of years ago at a party Marie dragged me to in an attempt to make me more social. I never wanted the attachment of a relationship – too many skeletons in my closet – but I have a healthy sexual appetite I like to keep fed. Mr. Walking Sex, now known as Nick, seems like the perfect specimen to feed my hunger. Would sex in the restaurant bathroom after lunch be too soon for that?

Finding a table at the local burger dive isn't hard, and we're quickly settled and talking small talk.

"So, Nick, what's your deal, what do you do?" I ask before I take a sip of my water, straight shooter and all.

It's a short hesitation. "I'm a cop."

Choking on my water, I stutter "A – a cop? How old are you?"

"Yeah, I've been a cop for about five years now. Actually, I recently made detective. I'm twenty-six. What about you? What's your deal, as you so eloquently put it?"

Playing it cool, I respond "Well, I just turned eighteen a few days ago, and I'll be finished with high school in a month or so."

Either my age will turn him off or he'll overlook it. It's not like I'm a minor anymore, but some guys still see eighteen as too young.

"Eighteen huh? Old enough to vote."

The waiter interrupts to jot down our order. We order our burgers and fries quickly, eyes never leaving each other's faces. I know it would be stupid to start something with him now that I know he is a cop, but I can't help myself.

We eat, and talk, for like an hour. No one needs that much time to cram a bit of cow meat down their throats. I say witty things like, "I never noticed you out running before."

When he smiles, I think I forget to breathe. He says, "I work a lot."

All I want is to eat him alive. I play it cool. Pop some fries into my mouth instead. I try to balance that with the fact of who and what he is. The word *cop* keeps popping up to the top of my brain. I push it down. I talk about anything else. I tell him some of the music I listen to when I run. "And what about you?" I ask. "Books on tape? Crime stories?"

He laughs and shakes his head. "I listen to the park as I run."

"All the new mothers with their strollers packed tight with bags of cocaine?"

"No." He grins. "Murderous squirrels in the trees. But maybe I should pay attention to some of those babies."

I haven't been at my best because I keep imagining he's handcuffing me, and I'm imagining it in both the very best of ways and the very worst. There's something enticing about being that close to someone who could fuck me over so badly.

I notice he's smirking. He's looking at me too closely. Behind his eyes, he's already playing with me. I lean over the table, which isn't really very close, and ask, "What?"

He holds my eyes. Doesn't look away like every other guy I've ever talked to. Nothing macho about it, just confidence. He says, "I thought you were cute before we came for lunch."

"And what do you think now?"

He's not grinning anymore. It's a real, honest smile. I can't remember the last time I saw one of those on anyone. Might've been Marie. Might've been never. "Now, I think you're cute *and* hot."

It's a good thing I didn't have a mouthful of beef and cheese, because right then I would've either spit it out or choked on it. Either way, I would've died.

CHAPTER FOUR

We didn't hook-up that day. Nick is either a gentleman or my being nearly nine years younger than him really is a problem. I have never been a very patient girl when it comes to getting what I want. I get it, plain and simple. I want Nick, and I do not care that he is a cop. Nor do I care that he was promoted from beat-cop to detective last year. Odds are he isn't a detective on the serial case. I just want to spend a night exploring all there is to explore on one another.

Some days later, realizing a cold shower just won't cut it, I go for yet another run. "Going to Hell" by The Pretty Reckless blares in my ears as I run towards Main Street. Hmm – I wonder if I really am sending myself straight to hell for taking the lives of all these men. Am I doomed?

Nah – no real God would send me to hell for killing slime who think molesting and raping children is okay. God, if there is a God, would send me to the greatest of heavens. If there is a heaven. Probably not, though, but whatever.

One song bleeds into the next and I just keep running. *I wonder how far I could get before it kills me*? Wow, that was dark. Where did that come from? I don't think I have ever thought about killing myself before; Marie's attempt to off herself steered me clear of ever thinking about that. It must be from the stress of Nick not wanting to have sex with me.

Maybe if I show up at his apartment unannounced and attack him, he'd have no choice. I mean, who can resist all this?

Aaaand there goes that cocky ego rearing its ugly head.

The spark I felt during lunch the other day was not all one sided. The way he looked at me with those eyes, he obviously wanted me. So why hasn't he called or come to find me? He knows the route I run; it's not that big of a town. Maybe he *doesn't* want me? Maybe it was all in my head. What the fuck is wrong with me? How is this guy getting to me so fucking bad? I need something to clear my head.

Finding a bench, I sit down and pull out my phone. Maybe if I find a mark, I can clear my head of Nick. Scrolling through the list I find one about five blocks away. Why are there so many fucking pedo-freaks in this town? Do men have nothing better to do than fuck with little kids? Letting out a frustrated sigh, I stretch before heading back home for my car. It's been like a week since Darell and the media has been strangely quiet about the whole thing. Usually it's all any news station in the area can talk about for days.

Jogging up the few steps to my front door, I get this sudden tingle up my spine, as if I'm being watched. Not letting on that I know someone is there, I pull out my key and unlock the door. Sensing someone behind me, and seeing out of my periphery a hand beginning to go for my shoulder, I grab the hand and twist around, putting the dumbass in a wrist lock. Just about the time I pin him against the door I realize he's shouting.

"Raven! Raven! Oww, goddammit, it's me. Dominick!"

"Oh shit! Sorry. So, so, sorry Nick." I release my hold on him.

"Where in the hell did you learn how to do that?" He rubs his wrist and rolls his shoulder.

"Just something I learned in a class," I mumble nonchalantly and turn to finish opening the door.

"Right."

I thrust open the door and walk in. He doesn't follow me in. He's still standing in the doorway when I spin around to face him. "Was there something you needed?"

Nick looked up, glazy eyed as if snapping out of a day dream. His hand was rubbing the back of his neck, while the shoulder I twisted let his other arm hang by his side. His mouth mumbled, incoherently, like I had twisted his spine and not just his arm.

I ask again, "Well...?"

His blue eyes clear and lock with mine, lighting something inside me that I never thought I could feel.

"I don't know if I should." He doesn't seem to want to look at me directly, but he won't stop looking at me anyway. "I've been having an internal war with myself the past few days. If I come in, I don't know if that's a win." He takes a breath before continuing. "Or a loss."

Leaning against the door jamb, looking all lost and confused, Nick literally melts my heart. I didn't think that was even possible. Before I have time to think and stop myself, I grab him and kiss him with all I have. After only the slightest hesitation, he kisses me back with so much gusto I feel like we might fall backwards. Pulling away slightly, I look up into his eyes. The raw passion there severs any plans I might have had for this to be a simple hookup. This is either going to end in rainbows and sunshine or a fiery crash and burn. I am all in, no matter the outcome. Only question is: is he?

Slamming the door behind us, we are all hands as we make our way up the hall. Luckily my mom is at work or this would be awkward. All the way up the stairs, we stumble and fumble, losing clothes along the way.

When we finally make it to my bed he stops, hovering over me, and asks, "Are you sure?"

"If I wasn't, we wouldn't be here." I pull his face back to mine.

CHAPTER FIVE

I wake up to him tickling the small of my back with the tips of his fingers. I have no idea what time it is, but it seems like it might be past midnight with how dark it is. Taking in the moment, I stay still. He is either going to regret this or not. I don't, and I am not ready to know the outcome. I have never felt this completely calm in my whole eighteen years.

"I know you're not sleeping," he says with a slight chuckle.

"Yes I am. I am fast asleep." I sigh and I roll over.

"We should talk."

And just like that, the calm is gone. Foreboding lingers in its place. I sit up and fumble for a shirt. Preparing for the worst. I don't know what to expect, but I cannot be naked when it happens. Trembling, I pull the shirt over my head and search around the room for some kind of pants.

Man, this room is a mess. I hope it isn't the reason for this sudden need to be serious. Not likely. This is something else entirely. I can feel him staring at me while I search. *Why is he just sitting there? I wish he would just spit it out.*

"I refuse to talk to your back, Raven. Turn around and listen to me. It's serious."

Sighing with resignation, I turn around and attempt to avoid his eyes.

"If you tell me this was a mistake, I think you might be the first person to ever make me cry." *Aside from my best friend.*

"It's only a mistake if you hate me after I tell you what I am about to tell you." Then he demands, "Come. Sit down."

I look up into his face. What could be so fucking serious? If he tells me he has some kind of disease, I will kill him. His face tells nothing. It's a mask of complete and total calm, cool and collected.

I sit at the end of the bed, out of reach. I can't let him touch me until I know what it is he needs to say. "Okay, talk."

"You...don't recognize me." He says it like a statement of knowledge, not a question.

"Should I?"

"I was the rookie accompanying Detective Rodriguez the night you were questioned about the death of your friend's mother's boyfriend."

And just like that, the bottom falls out from underneath me. Recognition suddenly becomes clear in my head. I try to play it cool, but I am sweating bullets and I can't breathe. The words come out in a rush. "What's your point?"

"My point is," he runs a hand through his hair and stands up to look out my window, "I never believed you were innocent." He turns back to look at me, "I have been secretly keeping tabs on you for the past four years."

"I see." *I don't.* "So what is this? Some fantasy you've been wanting to play out? Waiting until I was legal so that you wouldn't get charged as a pedophile?" I'm not thinking, just talking – and talking fast. "Afraid you'd have been next if you had?"

Angry, I stand up and walk towards the door. "Get out."

"Raven, wait. There's more."

I open the bedroom door wide enough for him to leave without touching me.

"Listen to me!" It's a whisper, but it hits me like a scream. He comes across the room and grabs me by the arm. He pushes the door shut and turns my body to face him. *"I'm the reason you've never been caught."*

He doesn't pause for long before continuing, but my mind is racing and I can't keep any thoughts straight anymore.

"I have been working to clean up your messes these past four years. And trust me when I say, *there were messes.* You almost always leave evidence."

I freeze in place; as still as a corpse after rigor mortis sets in. I don't know what to say or do. This is either a trap or he's psychotic. Both would be pretty bad. I decided to play it cool. "Let's say I understand what you're talking about, why would you do that? *You're a cop.* You should have arrested me four years ago. If any of this were true." *There, cool as a cucumber – not.*

It's his turn to sweat. I can see he's nervous. Why is he doing this?

"You're right. Honestly, I fought with myself about coming here today. It's bad enough being an anonymous accomplice, but to fall for you...and then fuck you...this is completely nuts!"

I open my mouth, but I don't get out any words quickly enough. He interrupts me. "And before you get your panties in a twist, falling for you just happened when we had lunch the other day. I had no inclination of feelings for you...until then. The shit just happened."

I think I should say something, but my mouth doesn't form the words. My brain runs a mile a minute trying to process everything he is saying– and not saying– yet my mouth does not form the words.

"There's ethics, right? Morals? I struggled with this for days. But I couldn't fight it. I couldn't stay away. You wormed your way under my skin and now here I am confessing everything to you." He let go of my arm at some point during all this. Now, he plops back down on the edge of the bed.

I have no idea what to say. What do you say to the cop that has secretly been helping you and has just got done fucking the life out of you?

I stammer. "But...but why?" I fidget with my hair, look around the room, try to find my words; I am so confused by his revelation. "Why did you start helping in the first place? That doesn't make sense." *Smooth, Raven. Just ignore the fact that he said he fucking fell for you. Get to the hard stuff.*

"It's what they deserved." He takes a breath to elaborate. "I hate the justice system in that aspect. After what happened to my sister – those fuckers should hang for what they do, but after maybe *a couple* of years in prison, they're released to do it again. It makes me *sick*."

Makes me sick, too, hence the whole vigilante shit. Someone has to make those assholes pay!

"Then there you were, destroying the very fuckers I wanted hanged. I didn't want you to go to juvie for that. Or worse, prison. You were a good kid with a good heart. And now...you're a beautiful woman. With so much passion and honor. Funny, sweet, strong. Fuck, Raven, what else do you want me to say?"

I can't breathe with him looking at me like that. Like I hold his life in my hands. What is he doing to me? I have never felt this exposed in my entire life, and I'm half fucking naked!

"I – I need some time to think. Clear my head. You...you're an amazing guy, but you have just rocked my whole world." Literally and figuratively. "I need to figure out how I feel, what to do, and I can't do that with you sitting two inches from me in a room that still has our sex haze hovering over it. So you need to go. I'll call you when I'm ready to talk."

With that, I kiss him one last time and stand to show him to the door.

He doesn't argue. He just walks out. I head to the kitchen to drown my sorrows in a pint of cookie dough ice cream.

What the fuck do I do now?

He knows. He's always known. How can I continue killing those sick fuckers and also get involved with Nick... who could ruin me in a heartbeat if anything goes wrong. How do I unfuck a situation that isn't even fucked yet?

My brain and my heart are warring with each other. Logic fighting passion, my passion for Nick and my passion for killing pedophiles. How do I continue to live in both worlds without failing at either?

I am so fucked.

CHAPTER SIX

I spend the next week in a haze. School, gym, home, bed, and repeat. No killing. No Nick. Just me, myself, and my thoughts. Normally I am constantly thinking about who my next mark is. But my days are filled with thoughts of Nick, what Nick said, what I said, what Nick's hands can do. My thoughts go back to the night together. The way his hands ran over my body, enticing shivers of excitement with every inch he touched. The way he kissed me – my lips, my navel, down to the apex between my thighs – like he was studying every inch of me and memorizing every dip and curve.

Yes, while dealing with this dilemma I am still thinking about sex. I have a healthy sexual appetite and finding out the guy I just fucked is my secret accomplice of four years, not to mention a detective, will not hinder that. I want those hands on me, in me, lighting me up again.

Needing a run and a change of scenery, I drive to the park to run laps around the track circling the playground. Sticking to my usual route might make me run into Nick and I don't know if I'm willing to see him yet. He has been very good at giving me my space, which makes me like him so much fucking more. What is better than a respectable man who honors your wishes AND is good in bed? Maybe a man that could've had you locked up anytime he wanted with evidence gathered for the past four years?

I freeze, literally, completely freeze in the middle of the track. There is no way he could turn me in after all this time. He would be implicating himself. He would go to jail right along with me. HE MADE HIMSELF A FUCKING ACCOMPLICE. Fucking idiot! Shaking my head, I turn and run back to my car. I jump in and start the ignition, then stop. *How the fuck do I find him?* I have spent this last week brooding about all of this for nothing. Nothing. And now, I just want to go to him, yet I don't know where the hell he is!

Going to the police station to scope out his whereabouts seems like the best course of action. When I find his car in the lot, I decide to wait for him to leave for the day. Four hours later, four long hours of ignoring and being ignored by the random people going in and out of the station, he's walking, with resignation, out of the station. I follow him home, at a distance so he doesn't notice me and become paranoid, back to his apartment.

Once he's inside, I get out of my car, walk over, and find his name on the wall of door bells. I buzz his bell about half a dozen times, bouncing up and down, impatient for him to answer.

I hear him through the speaker. "He...hello?"

"Let me in!" I practically shout. I jump up and down three more times before I hear the buzz for the door being unlocked. Running up three flights of stairs without getting winded is a serious feat that I accomplish quite well, thank you very much. He's standing at his door when I reach his floor. His rumbled hair and five o'clock shadow are so sexy I might die.

"Raven? What are you...?"

I slam my hand over his mouth and push him into the apartment. I kick shut the door behind me and say, "Shut up."

I push him to sit down on the couch and begin to pace back and forth. I haven't given this any thought and I almost don't know where to start. When he opens his mouth to say something, I put up a finger and look at him letting every emotion I feel show on my face. Stripping myself bare and laying down all my barriers and walls.

"My biggest fear," I start, "is that things would somehow get fucked up between us and you'd turn in four years of evidence on me and I would be fucked for the rest of my life."

I pause for a breath. He's smart enough to not interrupt. "But as I went running today, and running is thinking, and I realized there's no way you could do that. You'd be implicating yourself. And what kind of idiot would do that? Exactly.

No one." I'm pacing now. back and forth across the small space of his living room.

Another breath. He's so fucking patient. "So now my biggest question is simple. Will you try to stop me if we continue forward?"

I stop pacing and, in the middle of the room, stare down at him sitting on the couch. After what feels like forever, but is probably only a minute he stands and walks over to me. He reaches out to touch my face.

"What...what are you doing?" I'm nervous. His touch gives me butterflies.

"Shhh..." is all that comes out of his mouth before it descends onto mine. Giving in immediately, and completely, I wrap my arms around his neck. When that's not enough, and with his arms around me already, I lift myself into him and wrap my legs around his waist.

He carries me into the bedroom where he gently lays me down on the bed.

As much as I enjoy his explorations of my body, I have to ask again. "Dominick, are you going to ask me to stop what I do if we delve further into whatever this is between us?"

He crawls slowly back up my body and lays down next to me, grabbing my hand. "I can't predict the future." he says, "But I know you are a strong-willed woman who will do whatever she wants. I haven't tried to stop you these past four years. Hell, I've helped you. And as lead detective I will continue to help as long as I need to. If you stop, it won't be because I asked you to."

I sigh and roll over to look him in the face. "Did you just say you're the lead detective?"

"I thought I mentioned that to you before...?"

"No, you skipped that detail. So you hold my future in your hands." I look down at his right hand caressing my chest. "And currently also my left boob. There's nothing I can do but continue this spiral with you."

He turns on the bed, pulling me up to straddle his hips. Giggling, I lean down to kiss him. This will be the start of something beautiful or disastrous – or maybe both.

CHAPTER SEVEN

The days start flying by. Graduation comes and goes without me even noticing. Nick and I are completely wrapped up in each other.

"You know, I have been here every day for the past month. Practically all my clothes have ended up in your laundry." I'm sorting through it to bring to the laundromat. *Got to love sitting in the middle of the floor surrounded by dirty laundry–not.*

"That was the maniacal plan," Nick says from this kitchen where he is doctoring our coffee. "Make you fall in love with me, then steal your clothes."

"Is that right? So you think you've succeeded in making me fall in love?" He isn't wrong, I'm head over heels, as strange as that feels to admit. I never thought I could feel this way. I thought I was immune to such sappy shit. But here we are, practically living together in sexual bliss. *Could be worse: I could be pregnant.*

"Oh yes," he says. "That's what you whispered in your sleep last night."

I snap my head up, surprised by this matter of fact statement. I said this in my sleep after he tried his handcuffs on me? After he thought he'd secured me to the headboard, I showed him how easily–well, with just a little work–I could get out of them. I told him no cuffs could hold me for long, he wanted proof and I gave it to him. And then in my sleep I reveal this nonsense? I don't buy it.

Just as I am about to slam him with the third degree, he dives onto the clothes pile in front of me and tackles me to the floor, tickling me. I scream and giggle, all while trying to wiggle my way out of his grasp.

"Stop, oh my God, stop. I hate being tickled." I scream.

"Admit you're in love with me." He continues his assault, tickling my ribs, pinning my legs with his.

"Alright. ALRIGHT. I'm in love with you," I admit, breathlessly.

With those words he stops tickling me, grabs my face and says, more serious than I ever thought he could be, "I'm in love with you, too." We start to make out as if our lives depend on it. Just as things are starting to take a turn towards the good stuff, my phone goes off.

New Sex Offender Listed in The Area

The way Nick looks at me, I begin to wonder if he was lying when he said he wouldn't ask me to stop. I don't know if I could. This vigilante bullshit has become such an integral part of me. Releasing me, he stands up and walks back to the kitchen.

"Nick. Are you upset?"

"Why would I be upset? I said I wouldn't ask you to stop. I knew this would be something you'd continue." With a forced little laugh, he adds, "Not like I expected you to cease being a killer. I *like* that there's someone out there ending these motherfuckers. I need someone out there doing that."

That's a bit too earnest and too honest. I don't know where it comes from, not exactly.

"Maybe I hoped you would maybe take into consideration the *me* of it all...the *us*. That we could put the last four years behind us." He shakes his head. "Silly of me to think you might *want* to stop. Our future is largely at risk if you keep going. But no, I'm not upset."

I sit there, staring at him, chin to chest. He really did expect me to stop. As much as I wished it was that easy, it's not.

I stand and walk over to him. "Baby..." I wrap my arms around him from behind. Whisper soft kisses across his back. I try to find a way to make him understand. I *need* him to understand. But I don't have any words.

He heaves a big sigh and turns to wrap his arms around me, tucking my head under his chin. "I love you Rave, I do. That's what scares me. Before, I was all for you doing it. I didn't worry about something going wrong. I mean, I worried about your well-being, but *now*–now I worry about losing you. It's completely different."

"I understand that. I do. Really." I pause because I have to get this right. He's not the only one scared. Which is ridiculous. What possible reason do I have to be scared? "But...this is a part of me I cannot just shut off. I need to do this. If I don't, these pedofreaks are free to just roam about, destroying the lives of innocent kids as they see fit. Someone needs to stop them. And since the justice system doesn't seem to care enough, no offense, I have become the person who does. If you agreed with me before you loved me, I need you to remember that feeling, because I will not be stopping anytime soon." With that, I reach up to kiss his cheek and walk away to get my stuff together to leave.

I don't turn back to look at him as I walk away, I'm too afraid to see the disappointment I knew would be clear on his face.

CHAPTER EIGHT

I spend the day at the park reading up on the latest pedofreak to move into the area. His name is Raymond. Served four years for molesting his only granddaughter. Now he's out and free to do it again. God, I really hate the American Justice System. People serve longer time for being caught with an herb than they serve for mentally destroying kids who have done nothing to deserve it except be innocent souls. It's absolutely fucking despicable.

Before I jump on my internal pedestal, I head back to my car to prepare for the event. After checking that everything is there in my hidden lock box, I make my way across town to Raymond the pedofreak's house. I pass by once, twice, three times. He's home. His car is in the driveway. How do these dickheads afford houses straight from prison, anyways? It just doesn't seem right.

I park my car around the street overlooking the back of his house. No sense being seen parked on his street. I pull on my usual garb and jog, like I usually do, around to his street. I walk up the steps to his house and ring the bell with my sleeve covering my finger. As I wait, I think back to what Nick said about leaving evidence. I never left evidence. I have no clue what he is talking about. I always wear my hair up in a bun, so no stragglers are getting loose there. My nails are always cut short and I always wear gloves. I never vomit, my running shoes are generic and a size too big just to make sure if I do step in any blood, footprints cannot be traced back to me. On top of all that, I always clean the knife and put it back right where I found it without a print or drop of blood in sight.

Raymond answers the door. For an old guy, he looks pretty fit. But I am more fit. I give him my usual line about my car being broken down, must have left my phone at home, can I please come in and use his to call my dad to come get me. Like all the rest of the sickos, he falls for it hook, line, and sinker. I follow him into the house, closing and locking the door behind me.

Pulling my trusty crowbar out, I bash him over the head with it as hard as I can. He drops to his knees with nothing more than an "oomph" and I kick him the rest of the way down. Leaving him lying there, I go in search of a butcher knife and mirror.

It takes all of five minutes to gather everything I need and be back in the hall where I left him. He's still laying there, knocked out, but I can tell he's coming to. I grab him by the back of his hair and whack his head against the ground, just once. I need him to be out just a bit longer so I can remove his pants and berries.

As I viciously remove his grotesque male innards with a single flick of the knife, I lean close to his ear and coo, "Wakey wakey, Raymond. It's time to play."

"Wha...what the – aaaahhh, what the fuck?!?!" he screams and struggles against his ropes. His sounds are nonsensical and barely form words.

I wait a few moments as he struggles, squirming and pulling and trying to get himself upright. He's bound too well.

I lean over and, without a word of warning, ram the knife, sharp side facing the right, through his sphincter. I twist the knife with finesse, delighting at the sound of his visceral screams. Just when I'm sure he won't be able to stand much more, I froggy leap up his back, yank his head by his hair, and watch his face as I slice slowly across his throat. I relish the way his blood splays across the full-length mirror in front of us like a work of bloody art.

I drop his head to lay in the puddle forming on the floor under his face and go clean off the knife. Just business as usual. Once completely done, I head out the back door, slip off my hoodie and shoes, and run barefoot across the yard to my car. I hide my clothes in my lockbox and start the car.

As I am driving down the road, Nick calls.

"Are you done pouting?" I joke as I answer on

Bluetooth. He can probably tell I'm out of breath. Excitement more than exertion.

"Depends. Did you finish with your plans?" He still sounds mad at me. I'll have to find some way to fix that.

"Yes. I'm on my way home to shower from my run. See you soon?"

"Probably not, I have a mess to clean up before I go to work. I'll just see you at home later. I love you." I still find it annoying when he claims I leave a mess behind. But whatever.

"Suit yourself. Love you too. Bye."

I drive to his apartment to shower. I know I still have laundry to do, so I'll gather that after my shower and head to the mat. Just the usual domestic life I have been living this past month. I like it. It suits me.

By the time Nick gets home from work, it's nearly three in the morning. He tries to be quiet but I can hear every move he makes in the bathroom. After he starts the shower running, I sneak up the hall and into the bathroom. He's in the middle of washing his chest when I slip into the shower with him.

I grab the sponge from him. "Want me to wash your back?"

"Sure." He turns his back to me. For being so steamy in here, there's an awfully cold chill.

"Something wrong, baby?" I ask. I try to not tremble as I rub his back side slowly.

"Nothing. Just a long night at work." I am about to ask him to explain when he turns briskly and thrusts me against the shower wall. Pins me there. With one hand, he holds both my wrists. His thigh abruptly spreads my legs as he covers my mouth to silence me with the other hand.

"No more talking about the work we do," he says. "We tell each other nothing more. It does not exist. I don't want to go to work knowing what you just did and worrying if today is the day I can't cover it up. Got it?"

I can't speak through his hand. so I nod.

He waits a moment. It's a long fucking moment. Finally, he removes his hand and puts his mouth on mine. A moment later, I feel his dick.

It's quick and rough, frantic even, but thoroughly satisfying. We finish the shower and head to bed. As he sleeps, I run my fingers through his hair and wonder just how this is going to work. Can we really have a relationship with rules like that? Seems strange. And impossible.

Maybe he's right. Maybe I should try to stop. It isn't fair to him, not really. He risks everything to protect me from being caught. I think it's only fair if I give him the same respect. Feeling settled, I slip into easy slumber.

I wake the next morning to a text message from Marie.

Just Checking in. haven't heard 4m u in nearly 2 months. Am I still comin back 2 town 4 my b-day?

Sighing, I sit up and think about how I should approach this. I do miss her, but last time was just so awkward and miserable. Plus, I have been staying with Nick so much, my mother probably assumes I don't live there anymore–if she's even noticed I'm gone. I've even started looking for a job to cover my phone and car.

It would mean asking Nick if she could stay here. He's still asleep. I sit back against the headboard and stare at him.

"Stop staring. I can feel your eyes burning a hole through my head." He rolls over and doesn't lift his head from the pillow. He peeks at me through half closed eyes.

"Uhm–Marie just texted me."

He sits up and adjusts himself against the headboard, mirroring my position.

"Aaaand...?"

"And," I say, fumbling through the words, "she wants to know if she can come back to town to see me for her birthday. Meaning she needs a place to stay for the weekend." I take a breath because I don't really want to say anything, but since when do I hold anything back? "And since I've been pretty much living here, this is where she would expect to stay. Since I'm here.

After another breath, I say, "Stop looking at me like that and say something."

He smiles at that last part. "She can sleep on the couch, if you'd like." He kisses me and drops back to the bed so he can snuggle my hip.

I text Marie back. *Sure, can't wait to see you!*

Then I shimmy down to cuddle Nick a bit longer before getting up and preparing for the day.

CHAPTER NINE

Marie has her own car now, so there will be no picking her up from the bus station this time. She arrives at the apartment just before dinner Friday evening. I buzz her up and open the door to await her arrival up the three flights. As soon as she opens the door from the stairwell, I instantly notice a change.

"You dyed your hair!"

"Yeah. Red. You like it?"

I pull her into an awkward hug. "It's...different, but yeah, I like it." Leading her into the living room, I say, "Nick should be home soon. He called a little while ago and said he was finishing up some last-minute paperwork."

"So...you live with your boyfriend now? The one you met, like, two months ago?"

I can feel her judgement but try to ignore it.

"Yeah, this is his place. I haven't officially moved in or anything, but I'm usually always here. My clothes all slowly made their way here. And my toothbrush. And hair straightener..." My rambling slowly dies off on a misplaced giggle. I stand there, quiet, as Marie looks around disapprovingly.

But I can't hold back. "Okay, seriously. Why did things get so fucking weird after you moved?" It's like word-vomit. It just comes out on its own.

"What? I don't know. You're the one that got all weird and stopped talking to me. You get a boyfriend as soon as I move and suddenly I don't exist anymore."

"What the fuck are you talking about? You showed up two months ago, acting like you didn't even know who I was anymore. Our whole weekend was spent staring at our phones and wishing the weekend would hurry up and finish already."

"That's because you got all weirded out about the prospect of me making new friends and actually having a life away from you!"

Just as I'm about to throw back some asinine retort, Nick walks in with pizza and wings, silencing the argument. He looks between the both of us, senses he has walked into the middle of something, and heads to the kitchen.

I look at Marie and mouth the words, "We'll finish this later."

She rolls her eyes, pastes a fake smile onto her face, and follows Nick into the kitchen. She extends her hand. "Hi, I'm Marie." She wears that fake little smile only someone who has known her for her whole damn life would know as fake.

Dropping the wing he had already started

eating, he wipes his hands on a napkin and takes hers. "Hey! Dominick. Pizza?" is all he says as he picks up the wing and continues to eat.

"Uhm, sure. Thanks. Nice apartment you have here. So nice of you to let me stay for the weekend. Rave and I always planned to spend our eighteenth birthdays together no matter what. So here I am. She did tell you that we're eighteen, right?"

I can sense the condescension from a mile away. "Yes, Mar, he knows how old we are. I've never lied to him. Now would you knock it off? You're being rude as fuck."

At this moment, I feel deep in my soul our friendship is over. Ten years, completely down the drain. I don't know how we got here, but here we are.

Looking at me as if I've slapped her across the face, she blows her bangs out of her face, stomps over to her bags, and leaves the apartment, slamming the door in her wake. Nick and I stand in silence for a few minutes. I have no idea what to say.

Nick, being Nick, opens the fridge, grabs a beer, and as nonchalantly as he can ever be says, "Well, that was short lived. Pizza?"

I laugh hysterically. How could I not? He is so fucking adorable. I walk over, grab a slice of extra cheesy mushroom covered pizza, and kiss him hello.

"Thank you. You're awesome. I'm sorry about her. I don't even know who she is anymore. We used to be so close. And now, she's a totally different person."

"That happens when people grow up and grow apart. It's part of life. Want to pretend to watch TV and make out?" He wiggles his eyebrows at me and winks.

I shrug, "Might as well." We grab the pizza and wings and veg out in the living room for a while. Everything with him is so easy. Who knew life could be like this?

We spent the rest of the night cuddling and watching old reruns of *The Nanny.* Around midnight, we call it a night and crawl into bed, where I pass out pretty much as soon as my head hits the pillow. When I wake up the next morning, Nick is lying on his side looking at me.

"That's not at all creepy to wake up to," I say sarcastically while booping him on the nose.

"You know what? I've been thinking—"

"That's a dangerous concept," I say with a giggle.

"We never really do anything together outside of this apartment. Let's go on a date tonight."

I'm intrigued and slightly excited at the concept of an actual date. Scooting closer to him I lightly run my finger over his chest in a slow caress. Smiling shyly, I ask, "What do you have in mind?"

"I...don't...actually know. Uhm, dinner and a movie? Maybe take a drive somewhere and find a bit of an adventure? I hadn't exactly gotten that far into planning." He shivers as he says that last part, as my hand finds its way lower down his abdomen.

"Just say when, baby, and I'll be there." I crawl on top of him to straddle his hips and cover his mouth with mine.

I guide him into me as he grips my hips. We move in perfect unison. I sit up and ride him rough, like my life depends on it. He reaches up to grab the back of my neck, to pull me down to meet his lips. We move like that for a while before he rolls me on to my back and pins me there with his body.

Needing it to be a tad rougher, I guide his hand to my throat, wordlessly begging him to choke me. He obliges, with exactly enough pressure to give me the pleasure I'm seeking but not doing any true harm. In no time at all, I am riding the waves of orgasmic ecstasy, screaming his name as he thrusts one last time and blows his load. I swear I could spend the rest of my life fucking this man.

CHAPTER TEN

I got a job. No, not the slice and dice gig I have been doing, a real job—if you can call it that. I sling drinks at the local coffee shop making shit tips. But it's honest work that won't get Nick, or me, into trouble. I am so fucking bored with the Americano Macchiato Cappuccino bullshit, it physically hurts.

My phone has buzzed five times this month alone about a new pedofreak in the area. I have struggled to ignore it every single fucking time. I feel like one of those junkies. Drugs are being put right under my fucking nose and I am busting my ass trying to pretend they aren't fucking there. The things I am willing to do for love.

Unfortunately, I don't know how much longer I can resist. I need it like oxygen. Is there a support group for serial killers? Yes, I am that fucking desperate. Nick finds ways to entertain me when we aren't at work. But other than sex, nothing can grab my attention for long.

I know I promised to stop. But I can't help it. I

need a fix. I always thought I wasn't, like, *addicted* to killing...not an actual psycho serial killer...but I guess I am. All I need is just one last time and I will delete the app from my phone and get rid of all the stuff stored in the secret compartment in the car.

What's the worst that could happen? After all these years, I get caught?! HA! Seriously unlikely. Not with my boyfriend leading up the case. So why do I feel so sick to my stomach all of a sudden? Aaaand...here come those tacos I shouldn't have eaten. I barely make it in time to the bathroom when the chunks come flying. Gross, it feels like it's coming out of nose. Why does this feel like an omen?

Maybe I should just go back to bed and wait until tomorrow.

After about a two hour nap, I feel fine again. Probably was just the tacos. I flop down onto the couch to scroll through my phone and pick my next mark. As I am scrolling his details, making my plans for the day, my menstrual calendar sends a notification telling me my period is a week late.

All of the blood drains from my face. I feel cold and dizzy. If there was ever a time for me to be reckless and thoughtless, it would definitely be when I am riding the high of orgasmic ecstasy. No, no way...there is no way in hell that I'm pregnant. That would be insane. We've been together all of, what, four months? It's way too soon to be having a baby. I'm too young. No, I'm not pregnant, absolutely not.

I stand up, determined to continue with my intended plans for the day.

I feel nervous driving to my new mark's house. He lives in a resort area not far from the Oregon border. I never feel nervous, four years and over twenty kills...not a drop of nerves.

It's just the possibility of being pregnant. I attempt to push it from my mind, choosing instead to focus on the details I scrounge up about Mr. Frederick Jacobson. Two time convicted pedofreak. Teenage girls of about fifteen tend to get his berries in a twist. Served a total of eight years altogether for raping his girlfriend's twin daughters. Released about three months ago, he moved to live on his mother's old farm to maintain the land and house now that she's moved to a nursing home.

He's 48, not very old but should be an easy mark. Just stick to the M.O. and I should be out of there and home with Nick before dinner. No problem. Once this is done, I will delete the app and move on with my future.

The usual story of breaking down on the side of the road won't exactly work here because the dirt road driveway leading to his house is about a mile back from the road itself. I refuse to park THAT far from the house. So, I suppose I'll just have to go with "oh, sir, help me, I'm lost and my GPS isn't working out here!"

Parking in front of the old rundown farm house, I take a moment to collect myself. *Breathe in. Hold. Breathe out. I got this. I am strong and capable. No insane sicko can take me down.* I adjust my bun, pull on my oversized shoes and gloves, adjust the crowbar under my hoodie in the waistband of my track pants, and climb out of the car.

The further I get from the car, the lower the bars on my phone get, so I go back to the car to drop it on the seat. Just in case something does go wrong, I need Nick to be able to track me. How better to do that than with a phone with an actual signal?

I climb the six steps to reach the wraparound porch and ring the bell. Mr. Jacobson takes his sweet time answering the door. After about two minutes, I begin to turn away, thinking maybe he's not there after all.

He opens the door abruptly. "Can I help you, girl?" He eyes me up and down with a disgusting look on his face.

"Uh, yeah, so I was trying to find my way to a friend's house and I am totally lost. My stupid GPS just isn't getting signal out here." I'm bouncing from onc foot to the other and not meeting his eyes. "Can you help me? Oh...and also, I really have to pee. I drank like *three* Redbulls today."

Using my dumb young teen with no commonsense character feels like the right move. I want to appear underage and innocent, appeal to his senses so he'll let me into the house.

He continues staring at me with gross interest. Makes my skin crawl. Shit, I'm going to enjoy this kill. I'm still shifting my weight, but now it's because he makes me feel uneasy.

After what feels like an eternity, he answers me. "Yeah, come on in, I'll show you to the restroom and we can look up those directions for you." He's got a phlegmy slimy undertone to his voice. He turns his back to me and begins walking into the house.

I follow in his wake, quietly locking the door behind me and reaching under my hoodie for my crowbar. Just as I'm about to rear back and whack him over the head, he spins around. Latches onto my wrist with an iron fist and twists. Something snaps and I drop the crowbar, screaming with the pain. He pulls me towards him, so close I can see the spittle in the corners of his mouth.

He says, "Wrong one, little bitch." Then he head-butts me and my world goes dark.

CHAPTER ELEVEN

My face hurts. Why the fuck would anyone head-butt someone in the face? That just feels extra as fuck. Keeping still, I attempt to assess my situation. Somehow this went very, very wrong. I am tied up and splayed naked on a twin size bed. I feel him watching me from across the room.

"I know you're awake. The pattern of your breathing has changed. Without that bulky hoodie, you have a damn fine body. Your tits rise slowly with each breath, but now they're moving a little faster. I like that." I can hear the grin in his voice. He's been enjoying the show he made. Staring up my body from somewhere just beyond my legs. Fucking Pervert.

"What were you hoping to achieve here, little girl? Thought you would manhandle me? You think we ain't got the news in prison? I've done some thinking while you've been breathing there all passed out and shit. News has it all wrong, huh? Ain't some pissed off woman doin' all that dang killin'. It's you. Either that or you're a dumbass copycat." He pauses. He's walking toward me. I hear his footsteps. "I'm gonna have some fun with you, girl."

I figure if I talk, my smartass mouth might irritate him. If I don't respond, he might find that disrespectful. No one's ever gotten a jump on me like that before. I can feel how his hands groped me while removing my clothes. I'm definitely in a bit of a pickle here.

No, it's not just my flesh telling me what he's done. He's doing it now. Sliding his hand up my leg, taking his time as he inches his way towards my core.

Without permission, my body starts to shake. Trying to be subtle about it, I pull at the ropes at my wrists and ankles. They're too tight. My fingers are cold and numb. Fear, unadulterated fear, spreads through me. I have nothing left in me. No thoughts, no retorts...I am completely stuck. I have no idea how long I was knocked out for, no clue how I'm going to save myself.

All I have is the ability to not give him the pleasure of reacting. I need to calm my body down. Monsters like him can smell fear. I take a deep breath and hold it. In my head, I begin to sing, something Marie used to really like when we were in middle school, but I'm fucking up with words.

The bed creeks as he climbs onto it. The mattress shifts under his weight.

He's got his face buried in my crotch. Trying to make me feel pleasure. With his mouth. His sandpaper tongue. He knows that, despite his effort, he's failing miserably. Sorry, loser, I don't have any weird rape fantasies. I'm dry as Nevada.

"Why the fuck won't you cum?"

Growling in frustration, he raises his head suddenly and looks right at my eyes. I didn't even mean to be looking at the top of his ugly head.

His voice betrays his agitation. "I'm throwing all my best fucking moves down there. What, you like it rougher? Not into all that tender shit? You the kind of bitch that needs to be roughed up some in order to get off? Huh? You like that?"

He thrusts a hand up to my throat and squeezes. Cut off my airway completely. Pain radiates behind my eyes. If this monster squeezes any harder, my eyeballs might just pop out. He drags his body up my chest so he's basically sitting on my collarbones and starts rubbing his cock against my lips, seeking access.

It's not working for him. He jumps off the bed, circling around the top of it. The bed's in the middle of a room rather than against the wall. Knowing that is useless. Essentially from above me, he grabs my throat again, his big hand forcing my head back. His balls hang in my eyes as he shoves his dick at my mouth again.

I try to open it, despite being choked to near death in a vise-like bear claw of a hand. He tightens his fist around my neck for a moment, then lets up just long enough for me to gasp for air. The back of my throat is suddenly assaulted by his dick. It fills my mouth, pushing my cheeks apart. His choking hand slackens its grip as he thrusts harder, deeper and deeper. Tears fall hot from my eyes. I am in a hell worse than I could have ever imagined.

His hand starts jerking my throat within his clutch, as if the tight motion is masturbating him through my throat. After what feels like hours of this shit, me unable to breathe the whole time, he yanks out and explodes all over my face. He bends his head down to look at his canvas. My face. He's not seeing me at all and breathing heavily. I'm sobbing between deep mouthfuls of air. I'm shaking so hard, it almost feels like convulsions. Why didn't I just feign a fucking orgasm for the sick fuck when he was attempting to be tender? Feeling stupid, I cry even harder.

"Oh for fuck's sake, shut the fuck up, ya fucking cry baby! Ain't ya ever been skull fucked before?" He laughs a little. "Damn, here I thought I was giving you what you wanted. Thought you liked that shit, huh?" He grabs a shirt from the floor and roughly wipes away some of his disgusting juices. "I mean, shit, I didn't hear you saying no." He chuckles as if he's had a silly thought. "Now, you just stay put, I got something for your ass." Getting up, he walks over to the bedroom door.

"I'll be right back," he sings.

I don't know how long I have been here. Has it been long enough for Nick to realize something's up? I can see, from the window, that the sun is setting. The dim light casts an eerie glow into the room. It'll probably be another two hours before Nick starts to worry. Who's to say how long it'll be before he can find my location and come save me? If he can save me. There's no way this guy is ever gonna let me live. This isn't just a kidnapping and raping, this is a full blown *Bitch is gonna die* situation. I'm on my deathbed.

CHAPTER TWELVE

There's noise coming from the hallway, the fear racing through my mind, body and soul is suffocating. What is the next form of torture coming my way? Does he know what I've done to his fellow pedofreaks? Will he do the same to me? This is not at all how I pictured today going. How could I have been so stupid?

"Miss me?" he asks from the doorway. I don't look at him, but an involuntary whimper escapes my lips, leaving me feeling disgusted with myself. I am *not* a weak petrified little girl. Yet here I am, shaking in unimaginable fear at just the sound of his voice. The bastard is breaking me, destroying my strength...my willpower to persevere. I wish he would just kill me. I don't know how much more I can handle.

My personal monster walks into view and shows me a thick, long butcher's knife. "I wanna play," he says. "Do you wanna play? How much pain can I make you feel before you pass out?"

He smiles, and for the first time I notice he has

a few rotting teeth, and one missing. My severe A.D.D. leads me to wonder what happened to prisons having good health care. Before I can internally delve too far on that ridiculous thought track, I feel the first stinging pain of having the skin on my right breast sliced open.

Not enough to make me bleed out profusely. He doesn't want me to die too quickly. But enough that the stitches will leave a scar.

Refusing to cry out, I bite down on my lip. The coppery taste of blood pools in my mouth. I swallow it down, along with the bile rising up my throat as he laps at my wound with his tongue. It feels as though he's making out with the opening, as if the cut is a set of lips. His tongue wiggles around within the wound. *Sick fuck.*

I try to envision Nick's face, the way his smile is slightly crooked on one side due to having only one dimple on his left cheek. The way his eyes crinkle at the corners when he laughs. Anything to avoid the pain my body is currently enduring.

My monster has moved to my left breast, slicing it in the same fashion and giving it the same tongue fucking. I again try to find a happy place in which to hide away. Nick's body as he exits the shower in nothing but a towel, hair still dripping wet, beads of water glistening in the light splatter of hair across his chest.

Searing pain as he slices my abdomen.

Nick rubbing my feet after a long day of slinging coffee to the local hipsters. Whispering in my ear that he loves how, no matter how many showers I take, he can always smell the faint scent of coffee on my skin and in my hair.

Tears are falling helplessly out of my eyes. I am openly sobbing, giving in to the pain as he finger fucks the gaping wound on my belly. Please, God, just let me die.

Blood pools wetly under my back, soaking into the sheet. There is no way I'm gonna live much longer.

He's fucking me now. I can feel the monster ram his misshapen dick into my vagina, in, out, in, out, moaning with each thrust, sloshing through the blood.

"You're wet now, aren't you, girl," he says, not a question. The sound of him licking his bloody fingers makes me vomit in my mouth.

"Mmm...so tight. Feels even better than your mouth"

The bastard rams into me harder and faster. All I can do is lay there and take it, praying for it all to be over soon.

The day stretches past in a haze. I'm still alive, still going through hell, still begging a God that probably doesn't fucking exist to put me out of my misery. He's reaching his orgasmic climax, grimacing and growling like an animal. Just as his body starts to go rigid from the strain of cumming, there's a loud crack. I hear the sound as if it comes from a distance. I don't recognize it. Why should I?

I kicked him. Without knowing I was doing it, I'd managed to slip one ankle out of the rope, stretch the leg to my side, and bring it up. Heel connected with his skull just as he came. I don't have the strength to kill a man with a kick, but I do knock him off of me. Off the bed. Tearing his blood-soaked dick, still spewing, out of me as he falls.

The next sound is his head cracking the floor. Hard. Blood spurts like a fucking fountain. I can't focus. I'm not sure where the blood is coming from. Did he rupture something inside of me?

My leg drops to the bed. I can't free my hands. Or my other leg. I glance in his direction, which means turning my head and straining to see below me. Some of the blood is his, but he's blinking and his face is red with rage. He's pushing himself up again, slowly. I don't know if he staggers to one side as he gets to his knees or if it's just my eyes. I definitely can't see straight. I can't hear what he's saying.

And that's good. I don't want to listen to whatever he's got to say as I die. With a hand on the side of the bed, he pulls himself up enough to look directly at me. Blood streams down his face. He grins at me and it's the most sadistic shit I've ever seen. "I like 'em feisty."

Maybe he slurs. Maybe I just hear it funny.

But he definitely falls back when he gets to his feet. It's a slow process, rising, but quick when he teeters backwards. He closes his eyes. For a minute,

I think he might be dead. I pray that he's dead. Should I be praying? *Why the fuck not?*

And then, with a crack of thunder, he opens his eyes. All his eyes. The two in his head and the one above them, the red one, that wasn't there before. His body spasms and ricochets off the wall. He drops head first onto my chest. The warmth of his blood mingles with mine.

A scream exits my body just before the world starts to darken around me. I think I see Nick over me, shoving my monster's dead body off me. I'm obviously hallucinating. There's no way he found me. Maybe I'm going to go to heaven for all the deeds I have done and all my angels will look like my sweet love.

Yeah, that's it. This is my journey to the land of the dead. I'm finally dying, Mercy was taken on me, heaven here I come. Darkness finishes closing in and I shut my eyes, welcoming it.

CHAPTER THIRTEEN

There is no way this is heaven. Blinding light every time I try to open my eyes, incessant beeping, and unbearable pain slightly covered by a numb that can only come from painkillers. Either I'm actually alive or this is hell.

A hand lightly squeezing mine draws my attention from my internal debate of alive or hell.

"Wake up for me, baby, please. Just let me see those beautiful blue eyes."

That voice sounds like pure heaven, the sweetest voice I have ever known. I try to open my eyes, but the blinding light makes me wince and clamp them shut. Moaning in pain, I settle for squeezing his hand back, so he knows I'm here.

"Baby! Raven! NURSE! NURSE! She's waking up!" He pulls his hand from mine, leaving an empty feeling that brings tears to my eyes.

Please, please don't leave me.

A cacophony of noise across the room brings a painful shudder to me.

Too loud, make it stop.

"Raven? Raven, sweetie, I'm Dr. Milliron. Can you open your eyes for me?"

I try, and fail again. My throat is dry. Telling them to turn off the damn lights seems pointless when I can't seem to talk. It feels as if I have been in a desert without water for days. Settling for a whisper, I try to tell them what I need. "Lights." Cough. Clear throat. "Too...fucking...bright..." Cough again. Clear throat.

"It's too bright in here," my sweet angel tells the doctor. "She can't open her eyes against the light"

"Nurse, dim the lights. Raven, I'm going to give you a bit of water to help with your throat. But I need you to try and open your eyes."

Carefully, and slowly, I manage to open one eye, then the other. The first thing I do once I adjust to having them is search out Nick's face. There, floating impatiently behind the doctor's shoulder, is my love.

I hear the heart monitor pick up its tempo, betraying my feelings loud and clear. Nick smiles his adorable crooked smile, and I can literally see the wave of relief wash over his face.

A nurse brings water. I drink. I try not to gulp. It ignites pain in my throat as I swallow it but it feels so fucking good to clear the desert from my throat. "How long have I been out?"

"About two days," Dr. Milliron says, looking down at his clipboard. "You had us worried for a while. You lost a lot of blood. A transfusion was needed, along with quite a few stitches.

Unfortunately, the fetus did not make it."

Dr. Milliron glances up as a gasp exits my lips.

I feel cold all over. "Did you say fetus?"

A mix of shock and hurt runs through me. I knew it was possible that I was pregnant, but to have it confirmed and be told that, due to my stupidity and that bastard Jacobson...

I'll never know that baby.

My throat hitches with a painful and obscene sound. Tears fall from my eyes. I sob uncontrollably.

Nick comes around the doctor to wrap his arms around me. I can't even look at him. My stupidity means he'll never know our baby, either. I bury my face against him as tight as the pain in my body allows.

Dr. Milliron sounds quiet and more distant. "I'm sorry. I didn't realize you didn't know. You were two months pregnant, I assumed you knew. I apologize."

I don't look up or respond to the doctor. All I can do is continue to cry. Cry for my trauma, cry for the baby I will never have the chance to hold, cry for Nick, and cry from the pain. I hear the doctor and nurses exiting the room, but I don't look up. I'm too distraught with pain, inside and out.

For half an eternity, Nick holds me, rocking me gently, trying to comfort me. Eventually, my tears dry up. I feel hollow, like a shell. There is nothing left inside.

Nick pulls back to look me in my eyes like he's

searching for my soul. "Baby, it's okay, everything is going to be okay."

I know he's trying to reassure me, but his words pass through me. Nothing will ever be okay again. I pull away from him, doing my best to curl into a ball on my side, but the agonizing pain from my wounds and all the damn wires prevent it. The wind is knocked out of me from the pain. The skin on my abdomen pulls tight, feeling as if it is being sliced open all over again. I'm having trouble taking in a breath through the pain.

Nick understands without me having to say anything. He knows I need the nurse. He presses the call button.

"Can I help you?" a nurse asks through the speaker.

"I think we need more pain meds in here. She's struggling pretty bad."

A minute later, a nurse arrives with a syringe. Her badge says her name is Kelli.

"Hi, sweetie," she says, injecting the medicine into the IV port. "This oughta make ya feel a little better. It's Dilaudid. May make ya drowsy, though, so don't expect to be able to have much more conversation." She gives me one last sympathetic look before leaving.

Nick's got my hand in his again. He leans close to whisper. I don't even know if I'll be able to remember this later. "I want you to know everything's been handled. There's no evidence to give away why you were actually at that house."

He's rubbing gently at my palm in a soothing motion. "Your mom has been here off and on for the past two days. And Marie should arrive later today. She's extremely worried, Rave. We've all been worried."

All I can do is nod. Those drugs work fast, and to be honest...I don't really want to respond to any of what he just said. I just want to go to sleep and pretend everything has just been a nightmare.

Nick lays down beside me, careful not to pull my wires, and wraps his arms around me. The last words I hear before drifting into a drug-induced sleep are Nick telling me that he loves me.

CHAPTER FOURTEEN

It's a long week of healing, questions, visits, crying, and nightmares. Conversations with my mother and Marie are short and uncomfortable. Marie's carrying that doll when she visits. Ana. Clutching it like a prized possession. I don't think she's even aware of it. I haven't seen that thing in years. I think the doll is what keeps her from crying when she sees me.

The worst thing she tells me is she knows everything now. She remembers everything. She looks so fucking sad.

The questioning from the police is even worse. Nick has been handling me with kid gloves, and the doctors and nurses have been getting on my nerves, but the police want details I can't remember or simply can't give them. And every time it starts, it goes on until I absolutely can't anymore.

Finally, *finally*, I am being released. The pain is still there, internally and externally, but I am well enough to finish the healing process at home.

The nurse insists on wheeling me out to Nick's car in a wheelchair, claiming "hospital policy." Fuck their policies. Shit's fucking stupid.

Nick helps me slowly into the car, "Wanna stop for muffins and coffee before we head home?"

"Was that question ironic or do you really feel as if you need to ask?"

"Ironic, of course." Sliding in behind the wheel, he gives me a look, "Coffee and blueberry muffins it is, gorgeous." He puts the car into drive and heads to The Beanery, the coffee shop where I work.

We ride in comfortable silence for the ten minutes it takes to get there. I stare out the window, happy to be alive. Happy to have him at my side, but still feeling hollow inside. *When will this feeling subside?*

He leaves me in the car as he goes inside to grab our coffees and muffins. No way am I getting out of this car until we reach our apartment. I don't want to face more people and questions, the inevitable pathetic sympathy from everyone. I am not ready to face that particular burden of surviving just yet.

Nick comes out after about ten minutes and gets into the car. He hands me my coffee and puts his in the cup holder, dropping the bag of muffins on the floorboard next to my feet.

When we get home, he gives me his coffee to hold, as well as my own, puts the muffins in my lap, and scoops me out of the car. He intends to carry me up the stairs to our apartment.

"You are aware I can walk, right? Even if I am slow." I feel grumpy. The pain meds are wearing off, and frankly I'm sick of being treated like I'm fragile.

"I'm aware, but why walk when you can be carried?" He grins down at me in a way that melts my heart, breaking my resolve.

"Fine, whatever." It's not terrible, being carried by the big strong man that I love. "But I want to sit *on the couch* to drink my coffee and eat my muffin. I am tired of lying in a bed like an invalid. We can put on a cheesy movie and pretend this last week hasn't happened."

"Works for me." He opens the door to our domain without dropping me or upsetting the muffins and settles me onto the couch. He takes the bag and cups, puts them on the table, then takes the throw blanket off the back of the couch to drape across my lap. Once he's got me settled, and I don't resist, he sits next to me and hands me my coffee and the muffins.

It should be a long night of mindless movies and peace.

An hour into *Hallpass*, his phone buzzes in his pocket.

"Jessi?" he says into the phone. "What's wrong? Sweetie, stop crying."

I give him a quizzical look. He mouths, "My sister."

Standing up, he begins pacing the living room. "What do you mean, the bastard is out? He's supposed to be there for another six years!"

I watch as his entire body goes rigid from anger. This can't be good.

"No, no. It's okay. I'll come home soon. Don't worry. We'll get this handled. I love you too, Jess. See you soon."

Nick ends the call and plops onto the couch next to me, running his hands over his face. I've never seen him look so – tense?

"Nick, what's wrong? What happened?" Fear is racing through me now, whatever he is about to say can't be good.

"About six years ago," he says, pausing a lot and tightening his fists as he talks, "my little sister was at a friend's house for a slumber party. After her friends were all asleep, she got up to use the bathroom. On her way back to bed, her friend's dad stopped her in the hallway and brought her into his bedroom." His eyes are red. Tears aren't falling, but they're in there, waiting for an excuse to escape. There's also a growing anger. I've never seen Nick angry.

"He raped her, Rave. Viciously raped her. The next morning, when my mom picked her up, she was so upset it took most of the day for my mom to get what happened out of her. Once she did, my mom brought her to the hospital and got the authorities involved. The bastard was convicted and sent to prison for what should have been 12 years.

Turns out Jessi wasn't the only one of his daughter's friends that he had done this to. Two others came forward."

Another long pause. I'm not sure I should say anything, so I don't. Finally, Nick continues. "He had another six years to serve. But with prisons being overcrowded, the fucker was released yesterday for *good behavior.*"

He's visibly shaking by the end of his explanation, rage evident on his face. I know that look: he wants blood. That's the look I saw in the mirror years ago when I made my first kill.

Just then, everything clicks into place. "That's why you've been helping me all this time, isn't it?"

He doesn't answer right away. God, I wish he would look straight at me. "I guess so. Sick fucks like him deserve to die. No one should get away with what they do. Since Jessi, shit's definitely well deserved."

He sits up. Rests his elbows on his knees and drops his head into his hands. He speaks softly through clenched teeth. "That asshole doesn't deserve freedom. He should be six feet under."

"Where does Jessi live now?" I ask him. An idea is forming in my head.

"Back home, in Chicago. I always meant to get back there eventually, but everything here these past five years...time just slipped away."

He makes the decision himself. He's thinking the same things I am. "Guess I gotta go back now."

Nick sits up and looks at me. The thoughts passing between us fill the hollow feeling that's been plaguing me this past week.

I say it so he doesn't have to ask. "Looks like we'll be going to Chicago, then."

END

ACKNOWLEDGEMENTS

Thank you John for your guidance, friendship, and collaboration. Thank you to my big brother T.J. for his support and talent. The cover would not exist without your artistic hand. Thank you Lucas for your critique and friendship. Thank you to my best friend and Beta Reader Chris for pointing out the stupids. You four played a big role in the completion of my first novella. I couldn't have done it without any of you.

ABOUT THE AUTHOR

Born in Western New York, Miko relocated to Virginia as a teenager and has been there ever since. After over 20 years, she wouldn't trade that countryside for anything.

She has four insanely amazing kids that keep her focused and sane. She's even a doting cat mom.

She's been a fan of the horror genre since young, reading her first chapter book at age 7. She started writing her own poetry by 14. Her influences, besides Anne Rice, include Emily Dickinson, Sylvia Plath, and Richelle Mead. The feminine homicidal rage in this book had some Suzi Madron and Kelli Owen inspiration.

Well Deserved was a trauma-healing project that, after ten years of agonizing work, transformed into her first novella.

www.ingramcontent.com/pod-product-compliance
Lightning Source LLC
LaVergne TN
LVHW051012080826
845145LV00009B/2584